Dear Curly Hair

Author: Melodee Barnes

Illustrator: Anaís Balbás

Brave Brothers Books LLC
1389 W. 86th Street #186
Indianapolis, IN 46260
www.bravebrothersbooks.com

Dear Curly Hair

Twitter @BraveBrosBooks

Editor: Laura Boffa
Cover & Interior Design: Suzanne Parada

Library of Congress Control Number: 2020936702

Published September 2020 in the United States by Brave Brothers Books, LLC
ISBN 13: 978-1-952099-97-7

Dedication

To my mother who made childhood enchanting

And to my daughter whose curls are truly magical

Mya had tightly coiled hair. Whenever her mom styled her hair, she would sit still so her hair would be just right.

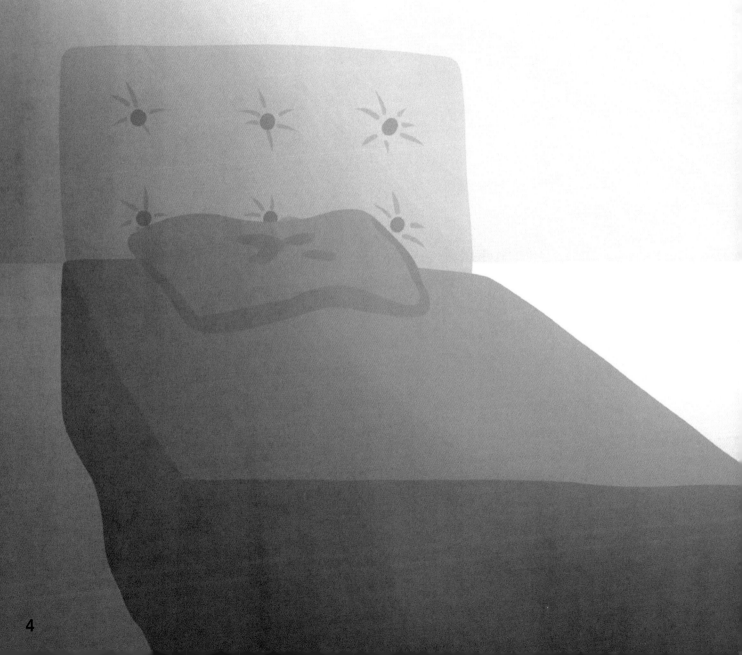

Mya's mom enjoyed styling her hair in different ways. Mya loved her free-flowing fro. Her curls would bounce when she walked.

5

Mya's mom would also twist her hair and place barrettes at the ends to hold the twists together. Mya's hair could do so much!

"Mya, your hair is so cute," her friend Simone would say.

"It really is!" Lynn would agree.

Mrs. Johnson always noticed when Mya's mom switched up her hair style. "It looks like someone has a new hairdo today. Your hair is beautiful, but it's no match for your brilliant brain, Mya." A smile would creep across Mya's face.

Class Rules

One weekend, Mya's mom washed and styled her hair. Then, she let Mya play while she whipped up some fluffy pancakes, eggs, and sausages.

"Mya, come to the kitchen. Breakfast is ready," she said.

"I'm on my way," Mya called back.

As Mya passed the television, a commercial caught her eye. "Make your hair shiny and new with this hair straightener called Honey Dew!"

Three brown girls twirled around, bopping to the background music beat. Their faces glowed. Their hair swung back and forth. Mya thought it looked shiny and smooth like the silk bonnet she wore at night.

I want my mom to buy Honey Dew, she thought. *I want my hair to be shiny and new, too.*

"Mya, your food is going to get cold."

"Coming, Mom," Mya replied.

Mya plopped down onto her chair.

"Sweetie, what's wrong?" her mom asked.

"Nothing," Mya fibbed.

Even though her mom had made her favorite food, pancakes, she was still thinking about the Honey Dew commercial. She remembered how the comb easily slid through the girls' hair in the commercial.

Mya thought back to earlier in the day when her mom did her hair.

"Whew, child! Let me add a little more leave-in conditioner so this comb will slip through your hair," her mom had said.

"Mya ... Mya ... Mya!"

The third time Mya heard her name, she snapped back to reality. She ate the rest of her pancakes and rushed off to her room.

Mya took out her journal and drew a picture of herself with straight hair. Then, she thought of a plan to make her dream a reality.

She quietly crept to the closet where her parents kept the bedsheets and towels. She pulled out one of her mom's silk pillowcases. Her mom slept on a silk pillowcase to help keep her hair from getting frizzy. *What if this silk pillowcase could be my hair?* thought Mya.

Next, Mya put the pillowcase on her head. In her mind, her hair was flowing just like the girls' hair in the Honey Dew commercial.

"Mya, Lynn is here. She wants you to come outside and play," her mom called up.

"Here, I come!"

Mya did not want her mom to see her hair. She grabbed her jacket with the hood, put it on, and ran outside.

"Hi, Mya! Let's play hopscotch with my sidewalk chalk!" said Lynn.

"Sure," Mya replied. Lynn drew the boxes for hopscotch, and they began to play.

"Why are you wearing a jacket? It's hot outside. You are sweating. Take it off." Mya paused.

She slowly slipped off her hood and waited for Lynn's reaction. She hoped her friend wouldn't laugh at her.

Lynn opened her mouth to say something but shrugged her shoulders instead.

The pillowcase was slippery. With each jump, it got looser. Eventually, it slipped off. "Oh no!" Mya cried.

"Why were you wearing that on your head?" asked Lynn.

"I wanted to look like the girls in the Honey Dew commercial," Mya said.

Lynn laughed. "I'm sorry. I shouldn't laugh. Your hair looked silly covered with that pillowcase. I like your real hair better," Lynn said.

"Well, I don't!" Mya replied. "I want my hair to look shiny and new with Honey Dew!"

"Your hair looks new all the time. You have the best-looking hair. All my momma knows how to do is part my hair down the middle and make two ponytails. I wish your mom could do my hair," said Lynn.

"Really?" asked Mya.

"Really," replied Lynn.

Mya reached over and gave Lynn a big hug.

"That's why you're my best friend! I think I should go put this pillowcase inside my house."

Mya held her head a little higher as she waved goodbye to Lynn and walked inside her home.

"Young lady, are you going to tell me why you were outside playing with my good pillowcase?" asked Mya's mom.

Mya held her head down.

"I was trying to make straight hair like the girls in the Honey Dew commercial. I thought my hair would look better like that. Lynn told me that was silly and that I have the best-looking hair."

"If I do say so myself, your hair is perfect," Mya's mom said. "However, there is nothing wrong with wanting to straighten your hair sometimes. Your grandma used to straighten my hair with a pressing comb because it made it easier to manage. When I learned to love my curls, I decided that I wasn't going to do that again to my hair or ever do that to yours."

"Come over here and look at yourself in this mirror. What do you see?" said Mya's mom.

Mya reached up and touched her hair.

"It's bouncy. It's soft. It can do so much."

"Did you know the curls interlock and intertwine together when I style your hair? Your hair can stay in those fun styles you like so much because of your curls. Your curls are amazing!"

Mya's mom looked her right in the eyes. "Your hair is beautiful the way it is ... and I think you should tell your hair."

Mya scrunched up her face. She did not understand what her mom meant.

Mya's mom pointed to her journal and handed her a pencil.

"Mya, you enjoy putting your thoughts into your journal. How about you write a letter to your hair?"

Mya wrote the first words, "Dear Curly Hair."
She tapped the pencil on the table
and thought more about what
she wanted to say.

28

Then, Mya smiled. She knew exactly what she wanted to tell her hair. "I love you!"

About the Author

MELODEE BARNES is an early childhood educator and has been in the classroom for over two decades.

Melodee is also the founder of Famly Nuggets, a platform dedicated to helping families become effective communicators and eliminate negative behavior. In her platform's name, there is no "i" in Famly because Melodee believes you cannot do family alone.

Melodee enjoys spending time with her children, watching romantic comedies, and serving in ministry for young people.

About the Illustrator

ANAÍS BALBÁS is a graphic designer and illustrator born in Venezuela. She spent most of her life in Puerto Rico, her mom's birthplace, and she currently resides in Orlando, Florida.

She studied graphic design in Puerto Rico, earning a bachelor's degree, but her passion is creating illustrations for children's books. She loves bringing an author's story to life through her illustrations.

Anaís also enjoys painting, knitting, and sewing.

To see samples of her work, you can view her portfolio at anaisbalbas.myportfolio.com.

Made in the USA
Coppell, TX
15 March 2023

14285088R00021